WELCOME TO RAVENS PASS

CURSES FOR SALE

by Steve Brezenoff

illustrated by Tom Percival

Ravens Pass is published by Stone Arch Books
a Capstone imprint
1710 Roe Crest Drive
North Mankato, Minnesota 56003
www.capstonepub.com

Library of Congress Cataloging-in-Publication Data

Brezenoff, Steven.
Curses for sale / written by Steve Brezenoff ; illustrated by
Tom Percival.
   p. cm. -- (Ravens Pass)
Summary: Jace Thomas buys a sleek, red ride-on toy car at a
garage sale in Ravens Pass, but when the car attacks him, Jace
realizes that everything at that sale is cursed.
ISBN 978-1-4342-3763-7 (library binding) -- ISBN 978-1-
4342-4209-9 (pbk.) -- ISBN 978-1-4342-4652-3 (ebook)
1. Riding toys--Juvenile fiction. 2. Horror tales. [1. Toys--
Fiction. 2. Automobiles--Fiction. 3. Supernatural--Fiction. 4.
Horror stories.] I. Percival, Tom, 1977- ill. II. Title.

PZ7.B7576Cu 2012
813.6--dc23   2012003958

Graphic Designer: Hilary Wacholz
Art Director: Kay Fraser

Printed in China.
I02016   010085R

Between where you live and where you've been, there is a town. It lies along the highway, and off the beaten path. It's in the middle of a forest, and in the middle of a desert. It's on the shore of a lake, and along a raging river. It's surrounded by mountains, and on the edge of a deadly cliff. If you're looking for it, you'll never find it, but if you're lost, it'll appear on your path.

The town is **RAVENS PASS**, and you might never leave.

TABLE OF CONTENTS

I HUNGRY

It was hot. Really hot. Jace Thomas sat in the passenger seat of his dad's car as it inched along the highway.

The passenger seat of his dad's car, Jace thought, was probably the hottest place on earth.

"I see trees, Daddy!" shouted Jace's little sister, Ruth, from the backseat. She was almost three years old. "Daddy! Look! I see trees!"

"That's great, sweetie," Dad said. Then he punched the steering wheel and shouted, "Come on! What's the hold-up?"

Jace leaned back in his seat and let his arm hang out the window. Dad's horn-honking didn't help. The traffic just wouldn't budge. They'd been sitting on the highway getting hotter and hotter for almost an hour. Jace just stared at the road sign a few feet up on the side of the road. It read, "Next exit: Ravens Pass."

Someone had spray-painted on the sign: "Turn back now!"

"Dad," Jace said. He fiddled with the vents, but it didn't help. The air-conditioning in Dad's car hadn't worked in years. "Can't we take the streets? We've been here for hours!"

Dad glanced at Jace. Then he checked the rearview mirror. Ruth was handling it okay, but soon she'd start fussing. She bounced in her car seat, muttering, "I see trees. I see trees."

"I don't know, Jace," Dad said. He patted at the sweat on his bald head. "I've never been to Ravens Pass before, and I'd really hate to get us lost way out here."

"At least we'd be moving," Jace mumbled. "A breeze would help cool us off."

Ruth said quietly, "I hungry, Daddy."

"Uh oh," Dad said.

"I hungry, Daddy," Ruth said, a little louder. "I hungry. I hungry."

"Dad, we have to get moving," Jace said. He turned and looked back at his sister. "Now!"

Ruth took a deep breath. "Daddy!" she shouted. "I hungry!"

"Here we go!" Dad said. And then he slammed on the gas and swerved onto the shoulder.

With the two right wheels of the car in the gravel, he sped toward the Ravens Pass exit.

chapter 2

THE SALE

"I feel better," Jace said. He and his dad walked slowly down the sidewalk of Main Street in Ravens Pass. They'd had a quick lunch of pizza and sodas. Ruth was sleeping happily on Dad's shoulder.

"Me too," Dad said. "I'm glad we stopped here. As a matter of fact, look at that." He pointed down the street. "A garage sale."

"Oh no," Jace said. He grabbed his dad's elbow. "Can't we just head home now?"

But Dad was already grinning and walking toward the corner. Jace groaned. If there was one thing he knew, it was that nothing—and that meant really, nothing at all—could keep Dad away from a garage sale.

Soon, Jace was surrounded by garage-salers. Ruth was awake and digging through a box of old dollies, squealing every time she found a new one she liked. Dad was flipping through stacks and stacks of records, making a pile of the ones he wanted.

Jace sat on a worn, wooden stool at the back of the sale to wait.

"There's some great stuff here, Jace," Dad called out. He held up an LP jacket with a photo of a dorky-looking guy in a white suit. "This was your grandmother's favorite singer!"

Jace dropped his head into his hands. "Get me out of here," he mumbled.

"Want to get out of here? I have just the thing to do that," someone said.

Jace lifted his head.

A tall, skinny man with thinning curly hair and a thick gray mustache stood there. He was smiling, or maybe just trying to. The man seemed out of practice at smiling.

"Oh, sorry," Jace said, jumping up from the stool. "Is this your garage sale?"

The man ignored the question. Instead, he lifted the table cloth of a nearby folding table to reveal a ride-on toy car underneath. He reached in and pulled it out, into plain sight. "Voila," the man said. "This will get you out of here!"

Jace liked what he saw. It was made for a kid a little younger than him, but somehow he didn't care. It was sleek and red, built like a convertible from the 1960s.

The seats even looked like real leather. On the passenger seat was a pair of driving gloves. It was the coolest thing Jace had ever seen.

"Wow," Jace said. He ran his finger along the top of the door on one side. "It's for sale?"

"Of course," the man said. "Why else would it be here?"

Dad walked up. He was carrying an armful of records and a set of five coffee mugs (labeled Monday through Friday). A white rabbit's foot dangled from his pinky finger. On his head was a baseball cap with a minor league team's logo on it.

"That looks expensive," Dad said, gazing down at the red car.

Jace looked at the man with the mustache. "Is it?" he asked.

"Let's see," the man said. He looked at Jace, then at Jace's dad, then back at Jace. Finally he knelt next to the little red sports car. "I'll sell it for five dollars."

Jace's eyes went wide. He quickly dug into his pocket and pulled out a crumpled five-dollar bill. His dad didn't even have time to think about whether Jace could bring it home.

"Here you go," Jace said, holding out the bill.

The man grabbed it and shoved it into his own pocket.

"Thank you," he said.

Then he walked off to talk to a woman who was looking at a set of dining room chairs.

"See if you can get that into the trunk," Dad said. "I'll pay for this other stuff and see what Ruth has found."

When the trunk was loaded up with the car, records, and other odds and ends, they headed back to the highway. The traffic was gone. They were out of Ravens Pass and back home in Lakeville in no time.

THE ACCIDENT

"Honestly, dear," Jace's mom said, watching Jace's dad lug another box into the house. "Do you have to stop at every single garage sale you see?" she asked. "Don't we have enough junk in this house?"

Dad held up a record with a rainbow-printed sleeve. "I thought you'd love this!" he said. "I bought it for you!"

"We have three copies of that LP already!" Mom snapped back.

Jace didn't feel like listening to his parents arguing about Dad's garage-sale habit again. He decided to show his new sports car to his friend Sam Lewis, who lived down the block.

The toy car was parked in the driveway, next to the last box of Dad's haul from the sale. Jace peeked into the box. It contained two dolls (for Ruth, he figured), the five coffee mugs, and the rabbit's foot.

Jace climbed into the car, started it up, and drove toward Sam's house.

"Wow," he said, smiling as he drove. "It works great!"

And it was fast—or it felt fast, anyway. The wind blew through Jace's hair as he steered down Juniper Lane.

Sam was in his driveway, practicing free throws.

"Hey, Sam!" Jace called, driving toward his friend. He skidded to a stop in Sam's driveway. "Check out my car. How do you like the new wheels?"

Sam whistled. "Pretty cool," he said. "Where'd you get that thing?"

"I paid five bucks for it at a garage sale," Jace said. He climbed out. The car really was too small for him, but that didn't make it less fun. "Wanna take it for a spin?"

Sam nodded eagerly. "Let me at it," he said. He tossed the basketball to Jace. Then he climbed into the car.

"Don't crash it," Jace said. "It's my pride and joy!"

Sam waved him off. "Don't worry about it. I'm a pro," he said. The car launched into the street. Sam sped away, laughing. "This is awesome!" he yelled.

Jace sat in the driveway, watching. He laughed as Sam spun out in the street. While Sam drove, Jace made a couple of shots with the basketball, and practiced twirling the ball on his finger for a while.

After driving around for a few minutes, Sam drove back into the driveway and parked next to Jace.

"Pretty good, huh?" Jace said, smiling proudly. "Can you believe it?"

Sam nodded. "It's excellent," he said. "I gotta start going to garage sales. How much did you pay for this thing?"

"Five bucks," Jace said. "Can you believe it?"

Sam laughed. "It's pretty great," he said.

"Okay, my turn again," Jace said.

"Oh, okay," Sam said. He started to get up to climb out.

But as he did, he slipped. His foot hit the gas pedal, and the car took off—fast—toward the street.

"Watch out!" Jace shouted.

Sam gripped the steering wheel and tried to press the brake, but the car didn't stop. It seemed to even speed up.

At that very moment, Jace's dad's old sedan came rumbling down Juniper Lane.

"Dad!" Jace screamed.

The brakes squealed in the big old car.

The toy red sports car zigzagged back and forth in the road as Sam tried to get control again.

Dad was forced to turn hard to the left to avoid the toy car. The big old sedan went flying into a lamp post.

Its front crumpled as it spun twice and tore up half a lawn before stopping—a smoking pile of metal and glass.

chapter 4

THE WRECKAGE

"He's going to be okay, Mom," Jace said.

They were on the way back from the hospital, where Dad would have to spend the night. He had a broken leg and lots of bumps and bruises, but Jace was right. Dad would be okay.

Mom was gripping the steering wheel so hard that her fingers were red and her knuckles were white.

"You're getting rid of that toy car," she said through her teeth.

"What?" Jace asked. "Why? It wasn't the car's fault."

"I knew it would be trouble the minute you and your dad got back from that dumb garage sale," Mom said.

She sniffed. Jace thought she'd cry again. "But it was Sam's fault, not the car's," he said quietly.

"I'm not going to discuss this, Jace!" Mom snapped, taking her eyes off the road to glare at her son. "The car goes, today!"

In the back, Ruth giggled. "Car goes!" she chanted. "Car goes!"

"Shut it, Ruth," Jace said.

"Don't you talk to your sister like that," Mom said. She pulled up to the curb in front of Sam's house. The toy car was in the driveway.

"Out," Mom snapped.

Jace grunted and threw the door open. He barely had a chance to close it again before his mom's car sped off down Juniper Lane and drove toward their house.

"There's no reason to be mad at me," Jace muttered. "You're the one who sent Dad out to donate all the stuff he bought."

He stood at the bottom of Sam's driveway and looked at the bent lamp post a little way down the street.

Most of the wreckage had been cleared already. Still, pieces of his dad's old sedan were still here and there, strewn all around the lawn and the gutter.

Jace walked over for a closer look.

He knelt down and picked up a chunk of orange plastic—a piece of one of Dad's turn signals. Jace tossed it back onto the lawn.

Not far off was half the rearview mirror. Jace picked it up and looked at his reflection for a minute. His eyes were still red and his cheeks were still stained from crying.

It had been a long day at the hospital.

Jace dropped the mirror. He looked down at it as it reflected the late afternoon sun back at him. Next to it, near a white-headed dandelion, was the rabbit's foot keychain his dad had bought at the garage sale.

"Dad will want this," he said to himself. He grabbed it, and then walked over to the toy car in Sam's driveway.

Jace leaned in and hung the rabbit's foot from the rearview mirror. Then he sighed and started to push the car down the block toward his house. He didn't want to drive it again. He pushed it right into their garage, next to his mom's station wagon, where Dad's sedan should have been parked. In its place, the little toy sports car looked pretty ridiculous.

Mom stuck her head into the garage from the door to the kitchen. "Dinner, two minutes," she said. She was still angry. Jace could tell.

"What are we having?" Jace asked.

As the door closed, he barely heard her reply, "Leftover tuna casserole."

Jace kicked the little red car, leaving a dent in the right side. The lights flickered on and off. The little rabbit's foot swung back and forth.

Jace watched it swing for a moment. Then he went inside.

"As soon as dinner is over," his mom said the moment he sat down, "that car goes in the garbage."

Jace picked up his fork and poked at the lukewarm cube of noodles, fish, and cracker crumbs on his plate.

chapter 5

UNDER ATTACK

Before long, Jace and Ruth were alone at the kitchen table. Mom had declared, "I just can't eat at a time like this." Then she'd gotten up from the table and gone into the hall with the phone.

Ruth immediately stood up in her chair and tossed her orange plastic fork at the refrigerator.

Normally, Jace would tell her to sit down, or he'd call for Mom. But that night, he just wasn't in the mood.

He stared at the door to the garage, worrying about his dad. "You think Dad's okay, Ruthie?" he asked, still looking at the door.

Ruthie didn't say anything. But to Jace's surprise, the door seemed to answer him.

First there was a high-pitched revving sound. Then there was a *toot-toot*. Then came the revving again, louder and louder.

Ruth stopped shouting and tossing utensils. She frowned, looking at her brother. "What that noise?" she asked Jace. She sat down and looked at the door, then at Jace.

Jace looked back at her and shrugged. "I have no idea," he told his sister. Then he got up from the table. He peeked into the hallway. Mom was sitting on the steps, talking quietly into the phone. Jace heard the words "insurance" and "disability."

The revving had gotten a little quieter, but it was still coming. Jace walked slowly to the door that led to the garage. He threw it open.

There was the toy red sports car, right where'd he left it. But now it was on. Its little engine hummed quietly. Its headlights were on, shining dusty beams across the dark garage floor.

"Why that car on?" Ruth said, standing up in her chair again.

Jace put out his hand to quiet her. Then he took a careful step into the garage.

The little car revved.

Its little engine growled.

Jace took another step. The car's hard-plastic tires scraped and squeaked on the cement floor, and it lurched forward.

Jace jumped back into the kitchen.

The car's engine hummed quietly, like a resting lion purring as it watched a herd of gazelles.

Ruth jumped down from her chair and ran into the hall. "Mommy!" she squealed.

Jace took a heavy step into the garage, hoping to shut off the car before his sister got back with Mom. But the car revved loudly. Instantly, it screeched toward him.

Jace barely had time to jump back into the kitchen and slam the door closed. But that didn't stop the car. Jace dove under the kitchen table just as the toy sports car smashed into the door.

The door splintered and flew from the hinges. Jace screamed.

chapter 6

POSSESSED

The sports car, its engine still revving high and loud, raced into a table leg, breaking it to bits and bringing the table down on top of Jace.

Then the car bounced off a chair, slammed into the kitchen wall, and stopped. The engine went quiet.

Jace sat under the half-fallen table, holding his breath, wondering if the car would start again. After a moment, he crawled slowly out from the wreckage—right into his mom's leg.

"What happened in here?!" she asked. "What in the world—"

Jace got to his feet. He looked at Ruth, hoping she might help him explain.

His sister had heard the revving engine, after all. She saw the car lurch at him, didn't she? The car had come to life! It had attacked Jace!

Ruth didn't say anything, though. She just sniffed and wiped the tears and boogers from her little cheeks.

Mom tapped her foot. "Well?" she said. "What happened, Jace? I need an answer right now. I've had enough."

Jace looked up at her, then at his feet. "The car came to life," he said.

"I'm sorry?" Mom said, shaking her head. "You'll have to repeat yourself. I thought I heard you say, 'The car came to life.'"

Jace nodded. "It did," he muttered.

"That's it," Mom said. She pointed at the staircase. "Go to your room. And I don't want to see you until it's time to leave for school tomorrow morning."

"Mom, seriously," Jace said.

"Go," Mom said. "I'm going to count to three."

"But it's true! I'm not lying!" Jace pleaded, his voice straining. "I didn't do anything! The car attacked me!"

"One," his mom said. She crossed her arms.

"This is so unfair," Jace insisted. "Mom. Please believe me. I didn't do this. I swear!"

"Two," Mom said. She put her hands on her hips.

"Fine!" Jace snapped. "I'm going, I'm going." He shot Ruth a glare, and then headed upstairs.

chapter 7

REVENGE

Up in his room, Jace fired up his computer, hoping Sam would be online to chat. He was.

"I'm glad you're online. I'm in big trouble," Jace typed.

Sam typed back, "?"

"That dumb car," Jace replied. "It started all by itself and tried to kill me in the kitchen."

Sam didn't type anything back for a few minutes.

Jace finally typed, "Hello?"

"I'm back," Sam typed. "I had to find a book."

"Why?" Jace typed.

"It's about a car that is possessed," Sam typed. "It kills people all over town, and eventually it kills its owner!"

"That's nuts," Jace replied. "It's just a silly ghost story."

"Stories, you mean," Sam typed. "There are a bunch of stories just like it—possessed cars, killer cars, owners who go crazy. I bet this car was owned by some kid who died, and he's haunting the car until he gets revenge or something!"

Jace leaned back in his chair. Maybe Sam was on to something. After all, Sam had lost all control of the car too.

Maybe the car had taken control on its own when Sam was driving, just like it had in the kitchen when it attacked Jace.

Then he got an idea.

"I need to find the guy who sold me that car," Jace typed into the chat window. "Maybe he'd know something about this."

"How will you find him?" Sam typed. "Do you even know his name?"

That is a problem, Jace thought. But maybe the man's name would be on one of the albums Dad picked out. Maybe he'd written it on there somewhere. Maybe there was still a chance to find out the guy's name.

"Hey, did you see my dad's car get towed?" Jace typed.

"Yeah," Sam replied. "My dad ran out and emptied the trunk before the tow truck hauled away the wreck. There was a ton of stuff from that garage sale in there."

"Perfect," Jace typed. "I need you to do me a favor."

chapter 8

MR. POPE

After Jace explained what he needed, Sam was away from his computer for a long time.

Jace tried to be patient. He even tried to take his mind off waiting by doing his reading for history class.

But after forty-five minutes, he couldn't take it anymore.

"Where are you??!" he typed into chat. There was no reply.

Jace quietly opened his bedroom door. He stuck his head out and tried to figure out where Mom was.

There wasn't a sound.

Maybe she fell asleep, he thought. *It's been a long day for all of us.*

He decided to take a risk. He tiptoed into the hallway, grabbed the phone from the little table at the top of the steps, and quietly crept back into his room. Then he dialed Sam's phone number.

Sam's dad picked up after one ring. "Hi, Mr. Lewis," Jace said. "Um, is Sam there?"

"Hi, Jace," Sam's dad said. "How is everyone over there? We sure had a fright today, didn't we?"

"Yes," Jace said. "We're okay. Dad's going to be fine."

"Good, good," Mr. Lewis said. "I'll see what Sam is up to. He was digging through your dad's latest music purchases last time I saw him. I think he's still at it."

A moment later, Sam came to the phone. He was out of breath when he said, "Hello?"

"Did you find anything?" Jace asked. "I've been waiting forever."

"Not forever," Sam said. "It's been forty-five minutes."

"So?" Jace said. "What did you find?"

"I found the man's name and his home address," Sam said. "It was written on one of those records."

"What?!" Jace said. "Why didn't you tell me?"

"I was still looking for a phone number," Sam said.

Jace rolled his eyes. "I'm sure I can find the guy's phone number if you tell me his name and address," he said. "Type it into chat." And he hung up.

He watched the screen.

After a few seconds, the information appeared in the chat window: "Christopher Pope, 234 Main Street, Ravens Pass."

Jace copied the text, pasted it into Google, and hit enter.

"I didn't know you bought your new car in Ravens Pass," Sam typed. "That place is freaky. I've heard a ton of really weird stories about that town."

Jace ignored the chat window and looked at the search results instead.

Christopher Pope's phone number appeared.

Jace grabbed the phone and dialed quickly, before he lost his nerve.

"Hello?" said a voice. Jace recognized the voice right away. It was definitely the tall old man who'd sold him the toy car.

"H-hello, Mr. Pope," Jace said. "Um, this is going to sound weird."

"Whatever it is," Mr. Pope said, "I'm not interested. If you need money, ask your momma. Goodbye!"

"Wait!" Jace shouted. "It's about the car!"

There was no click. Jace waited. But Mr. Pope didn't say anything.

"Are you still there?" Jace asked hopefully. "Mr. Pope?"

"What car?" Mr. Pope finally asked. "What are you talking about?"

"The toy car," Jace said. "The red one. The really cool one. I bought it at your garage sale this afternoon for five bucks."

"Hm," Mr. Pope said. "Right. The toy car. Okay, what about it? No returns. Buyer beware. All that stuff."

"Oh, I don't want my money back," Jace said.

I probably should *get my money back,* he thought, but he didn't bother saying that out loud. Five dollars seemed like nothing with a possessed car crashed in his kitchen, and his dad in the hospital because of it.

"I just wanted to ask you about the car," Jace said. "Did it ever seem weird?"

"What are you talking about?" Mr. Pope snapped. "I don't have time for this kind of malarkey. The news is on!"

"I mean, did anyone ever get hurt in it?" Jace said. "Like, seriously hurt?"

"Like who?" Mr. Pope said.

"Well, whose car was it?" Jace asked.

"It was my son's," Mr. Pope said.

"Did he die?" Jace asked. "Did the car kill him?"

"What in blazes are you talking about?" Mr. Pope said. "My son is nearly thirty, and he lives in Pine Bluff with his wife and three children."

"Oh," Jace said.

Somehow, he was disappointed. He felt stupid, too.

How could he have actually believed that a car could be possessed? It was probably just broken—bad wiring or something. His mom was right. It belonged at the dump.

"Sorry I bothered you," Jace said.

Mr. Pope snorted and hung up the phone.

Jace hung up too, and typed into chat what had happened. He finished by typing, "So I guess he never noticed anything strange about the car. Maybe it's an electrical problem or something."

"Mr. Pope was lying," Sam typed back right away.

Jace scratched his head. "How do you know?" he typed.

Sam sent a link. It led Jace to a newspaper article on the Ravens Pass newspaper website.

The article was very short. It was about a little girl who had died in Ravens Pass over twenty years ago. Her name was Christina Pope.

"Do you think this is Mr. Pope's daughter?" Jace typed into chat.

"Must be," Sam replied. "I bet she had an accident with that toy car."

"But the article doesn't say anything about a toy car," Jace typed. "I mean, what's the connection? Maybe she just died."

"Details, details," Sam replied. "There's no way it's just a coincidence. We have to destroy that car, before it can kill again."

Jace took a deep breath. "I'll have to sneak out," he typed. "Meet me in my driveway in five minutes. Bring your wagon."

"I'll be there," Sam wrote back.

"And be quiet," Jace added. "I'm pretty much grounded."

chapter 9

DEAD MAN'S HILL

Jace crouched at the foot of his driveway. The car, with its battery disconnected and sitting in the driver's seat, was next to him.

Jace stayed in the deep shadow of the big elm. It blocked all the light from the streetlamps, hiding him. His mom would go crazy if she discovered he'd left his room, never mind the house itself.

"Where is Sam? Why is he always late?" he muttered to himself.

Then he heard the distinctive sound of Sam's wagon wheels, squeaking and bumping up Juniper Lane.

"Finally," Jace whispered into the darkness.

"Sorry," Sam said, a little too loud. "I had to wait for my dad to finish working in the garage, so I could get the wagon."

"It's okay, let's go," Jace said. He lifted the back of the little car. "You get the front," he said.

Sam shook his head. "Uh-uh," he said. "I'm not touching that thing. I don't want to die."

Jace rolled his eyes. "Fine," he said.

He hefted the car into the wagon. Then he led the way.

It was a long walk, and the car seemed to get heavier and heavier as they went.

The wagon got harder to pull. The last quarter mile seemed to be straight up. But finally, they reached the top of Dead Man's Hill.

"Here we are," Jace said. He leaned as far as he would risk and peered down at the rocky shores of the lake. It looked like it was a mile down.

"Now what?" Sam asked.

"Now we push the car off the cliff," Jace said. "It smashes to bits on the rocks, we go home, and we never talk about this evil car again."

"Good plan," Sam said.

Jace tumbled the car out of the wagon and set it on its wheels at the edge of the cliff.

Sam frowned. "I wonder why it's not, like, trying to escape," he said.

"I took the battery out," Jace said.

Sam shrugged. "I didn't think that would stop it," he said. "If it's evil or whatever."

Jace looked at the car, wondering if it was about to spring to life and try to drive off. "Maybe it's sleeping," he said. Then he put one foot on the back of the car. He took a deep breath and shoved with all his might.

The red toy sports car soared off the cliff. For an instant, it looked like it would fly off over the lake. But then it just fell, only a few feet away from the edge. Both boys peered over the cliff to watch it hit the rocks.

It smashed to bits. Pieces of plastic and metal flew in all directions. The car was no more.

chapter 10

A CLOSE CALL

NFT. YTO. 3-YR.   NFT YTD 3-Y

Jace slept terribly that night. Though he was exhausted on the long walk home, when he finally got into bed he couldn't stop thinking about the possessed car.

He tossed and turned. When he did fall asleep, it was only briefly. His dreams were haunted by flashing headlights, tinny horn sounds, revving engines, and shattering tables and doors.

He shot awake as soon as his alarm went off the next morning.

"Wake up, Jace," his mom called through the door. "You're coming with me to pick up your father."

"But it's a school day," he called back. He got up and searched through the clothes on the floor for a pair of shorts.

"You'll be late," she said. "Now get dressed and downstairs."

Jace stumbled into the kitchen a few minutes later. He was tired and yawning. The table was gone. The whole mess had been cleaned up.

"Well, I guess we need a new table," he said.

His mom glared at him over the top of her coffee mug. "We'll talk about that later," she said. "And don't mention it to your dad. He has enough trouble right now."

Jace, his mom, and Ruth got in the car. As they started down Juniper Lane, heading to the hospital, Mom cleared her throat.

"You snuck out last night," she said quietly.

Jace froze.

"It's okay," she said. "I know you were getting rid of the car, and I appreciate that you did."

"Thanks," Jace said. "I mean, you're welcome. I mean, well, you know what I mean."

She glanced at him and smiled. Jace relaxed against the seat back. Ruth kicked his seat, but it didn't bother him. His dad was coming home, that car was gone, and everything would be back to normal now.

Then he noticed something dangling from the rearview mirror.

"Where'd that come from?" he asked, sitting up.

Mom smiled. "Do you like it?" she said.

She reached out and wrapped her fingers gently around the rabbit's foot. She stroked its short fur.

"I found it in the wreckage under the kitchen table," she said. "I think we could use some good luck after the last couple of days, don't you?"

"It was in the car," Jace said in a whisper.

"What are you talking about, honey?" Mom said.

"The rabbit's foot," he said.

"Oh?" Mom replied. She clicked on the right-turn signal as they approached the corner of Juniper Lane and Lake Street.

Jace nodded. "And it was in Dad's car when . . . ," he said.

He grabbed for the rabbit's foot, knocking his mom's hand out of the way.

"Jace!" she snapped.

Jace tore it from the mirror. On the tiny metal band at the chain end of the foot was an inscription: Christina Rose Pope.

Mom swerved as she took the turn onto Lake Street. The car lurched toward a lamppost. She tried to steer it back onto the right side of the road. She slammed on the brake pedal, but the car only sped up.

Ruth shrieked.

Jace pressed the button to open his window. It didn't budge. He stabbed it over and over, but nothing happened.

The car got faster and faster.

It sped down Lake Street, veering in and out of oncoming traffic.

Mom desperately tried to control the car, to stop it, to keep it from crashing with a car going in the other direction.

"I can't stop!" Mom shouted.

Jace pulled the handle, trying to open his door. Then he remembered the lock. He flipped the lock open as the car sped off the ramp, toward the woods on the edge of the highway.

The door handle resisted. With a grunt, Jace forced the door open. He tossed the rabbit's foot out and watched it land in the gutter.

At that moment, the car screeched to a stop, inches from a streetlight.

Jace slammed his door closed. "Drive," he said.

Several cars had stopped, and their drivers watched as Mom put the car in gear and slowly eased back into traffic.

"I don't understand," Mom said. She glanced at Jace. "Maybe you can explain it to me."

Jace sighed. "You wouldn't believe it," he said.

"Try me," Mom said.

chapter 11

THE END?

Just a few moments later, Sam Lewis was walking to school along Lake Street. He'd heard the screeching tires and honking horns, but he didn't know it was his friend's family. Noises like that came from a busy street like Lake Street all the time.

"I wonder where Jace is," he muttered to himself. He'd waited on the corner for a few minutes, since he and his friend usually walked to school together.

Sam kicked a stone as he walked. He often did when he walked to school. It made the walk more interesting.

He had a game he played when he kicked rocks. He'd see how far he could keep one stone going. If he could get it all the way to the front of the middle school, it would mean he'd have a good day.

Sam was a little superstitious sometimes.

That morning, though, he made one wrong kick, and the stone slipped off the sidewalk and the curb. It fell right into the gutter.

"Shoot," he said.

Sam hurried to the curb. Maybe he could kick the rock back up onto the sidewalk to keep going.

But what he saw was better luck than any stone would be.

There, a little muddy from the old rainwater in the gutter, was a rabbit's foot.

The chain was broken, but Sam knew that the luck didn't come from the chain. It came from the foot.

Sam picked it up, wiped off the mud with his fingers, and slipped it into his pocket.

ABOUT THE AUTHOR

STEVE BREZENOFF is the author of dozens of chapter books for young readers and two novels for young adults. Some of his creepiest ideas show up in dreams, so most of the Ravens Pass stories were written in his pajamas. He lives in St. Paul, Minnesota, with his wife and their son.

ABOUT THE ILLUSTRATOR

TOM PERCIVAL was born and raised in the wilds of Shropshire, England, a place of such remarkable natural beauty that Tom decided to sit in his room every day, drawing pictures and writing stories. But that was all a long time ago, and much has changed since then. Now, Tom lives in Bristol, England, where he sits in his room all day, drawing pictures and writing stories while his patient girlfriend, Liz, and their son, Ethan, keep him company.

GLOSSARY

CONNECTION (kuh-NEK-shuhn)—a link between two things

DISTINCTIVE (diss-TINGK-tiv)—making a person or thing different from all others

HABIT (HAB-it)—something that you do regularly, often without thinking about it

LP (ELL PEE)—short for long-playing, a record album

LUKEWARM (LUKE-worm)—slightly warm

MALARKEY (muh-LAR-kee)—nonsense

POSSESSED (puh-ZEST)—inhabited by an evil spirit

REVVING (REV-ing)—making an engine run quickly

SUPERSTITIOUS (soo-pur-STI-shuhss)—believing that some action not connected to a future event can influence the outcome of the event

WRECKAGE (REK-ij)—the broken parts or pieces lying around at the site of a crash or explosion

DISCUSSION QUESTIONS

1. Do you believe that objects can have good or bad luck attached to them? Why or why not?

2. In this series, Ravens Pass is a town where crazy things happen. Has anything spooky or creepy ever happened in your town? Talk about stories you know.

3. Can you think of any other explanations for the creepy things that happen in this book? Discuss your ideas.

WRITING PROMPTS

1. What happens next? Write a short story that extends this book.

2. Imagine something in your home is possessed. What object is it? What does it do? Write about it.

3. Write a newspaper article describing the events in this book.

THE CROW'S

A KILLER CAR COINCIDENCE?

Remember Christina Pope? Everybody said her death twenty years ago was an accident, but we here at the *Crow's Eye* never thought so. And now we have reason to believe we were right.

After all, Old Man Pope—Christina's dad—just had a garage sale, and then we heard through the grapevine that one of the items sold there had started acting up.

Here's what I know. Seems like a family from out of town stopped into Pope's sale. They bought a bunch of records, some old coffee mugs, and an old toy car, the kind a kid rides around in. I guess a thirteen-year-old boy picked that out.

So later that evening, the kid's dad gets into an accident. The next day, there's some kind of weird structural damage in the kid's house. And then the toy car ends up at the bottom of Dead Man's Hill, smashed to bits. I haven't heard anything else, but I know I will.

So, readers, what are we supposed to think? I'll tell you what they want us to think. They want us to think it was all coincidence. But I know better than that.

This is Ravens Pass. Nothing that happens here is a coincidence.

Old Man Pope's house the day of the garage sale.

MORE DARK TALES

WITCH MAYOR

There's a story going around that the mayor of Ravens Pass is a witch. Could it be true?

CURSES FOR SALE

Weird things happen after Jace buys an old toy car at a garage sale. Is the toy cursed?

FROM RAVENS PASS

THE SLEEPER

The old orphanage on the outskirts of Ravens Pass? It's full of aliens ready to take over the planet.

NEW IN TOWN

When Andy is threatened, a new kid protects him. But there's something very strange about the new kid in town . . .